For Rory, Peter and Brian

PHILOMEL BOOKS

A division of Penguin Young Readers Group.

Published by The Penguin Group.

Penguin Group (USA) Inc., 375 Hudson Street, New York, NY 10014, U.S.A.
Penguin Group (Canada), 90 Eglinton Avenue East, Suite 700, Toronto, Ontario, Canada M4P 2Y3
(a division of Pearson Penguin Canada Inc.)
Penguin Books Ltd, 80 Strand, London WC2R 0RL, England.
Penguin Ireland, 25 St. Stephen's Green, Dublin 2, Ireland (a division of Penguin Books Ltd.)
Penguin Group (Australia), 250 Camberwell Road, Camberwell, Victoria 3124, Australia
(a division of Pearson Australia Group Pty Ltd).
Penguin Books India Pvt Ltd, 11 Community Centre, Panchsheel Park, New Delhi - 110 017, India.
Penguin Group (NZ), Cnr Airborne and Rosedale Roads, Albany, Auckland 1310, New Zealand
(a division of Pearson New Zealand Ltd).
Penguin Books (South Africa) (Pty) Ltd, 24 Sturdee Avenue, Rosebank, Johannesburg 2196, South Africa.
Penguin Books Ltd, Registered Offices: 80 Strand, London WC2R 0RL, England.

Manufactured in China. The art for this book was created with watercolors on paper.

Library of Congress Cataloging-in-Publication Data

Jeffers, Oliver. Lost and found / Oliver Jeffers.—1st American ed. p. cm.
Summary: While trying his best to help a penguin that has shown up at his door,
a boy journeys all the way to the South Pole, only to realize that the penguin was never lost.
[1. Penguins—Fiction. 2. Lost and found possessions—Fiction. 3. Friendship—Fiction.
4. Voyages and travels—Fiction.] I. Title.
PZ7.J3643Los 2006 [E]—dc22 2005013520

ISBN 978-0-399-24503-9

14

Lost and Found

Oliver Jeffers

Philomel Books

Once there was a boy

who found a penguin at his door.

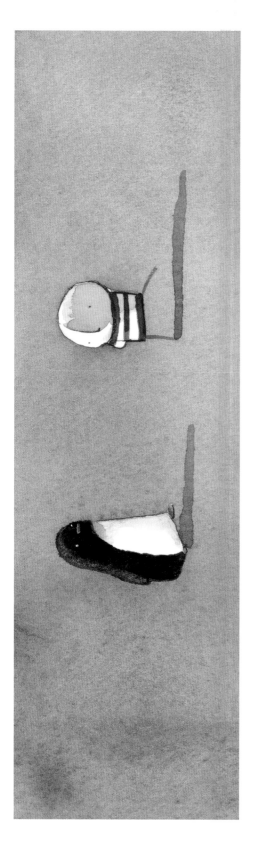

The boy didn't know where it had come from,

but it began to follow him everywhere.

The penguin looked sad and the boy thought it must be lost.

So the boy decided to help the penguin

find its way home.

He checked in the Lost and Found Office.

But no one was missing a penguin.

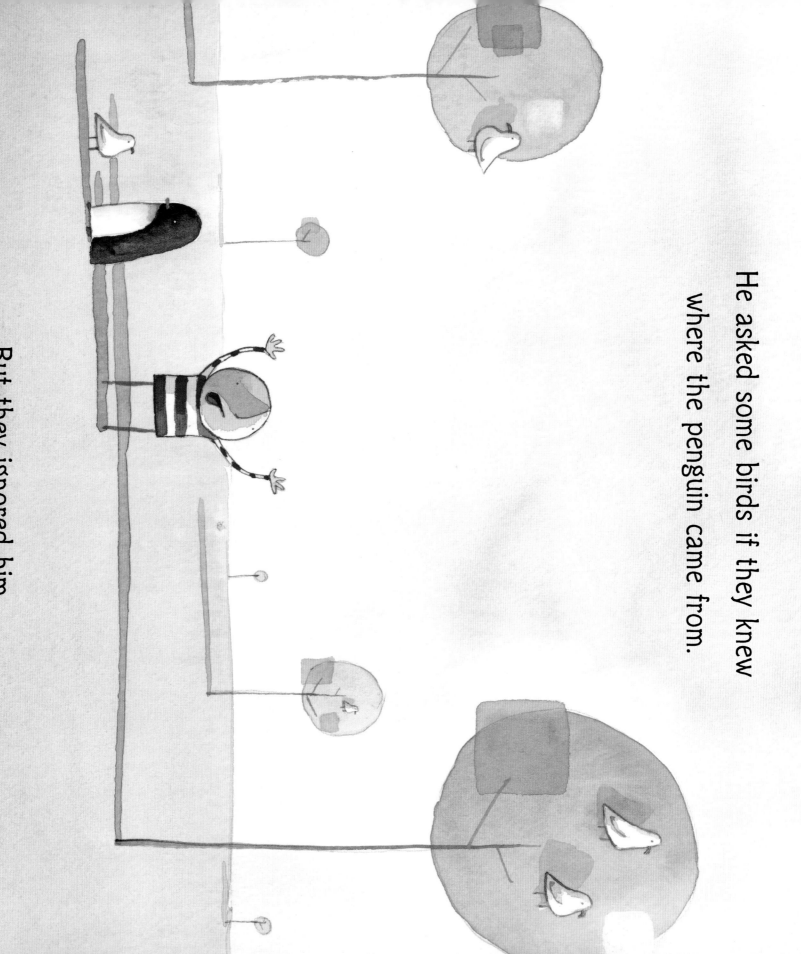

He asked some birds if they knew
where the penguin came from.

But they ignored him.
Some birds are like that.

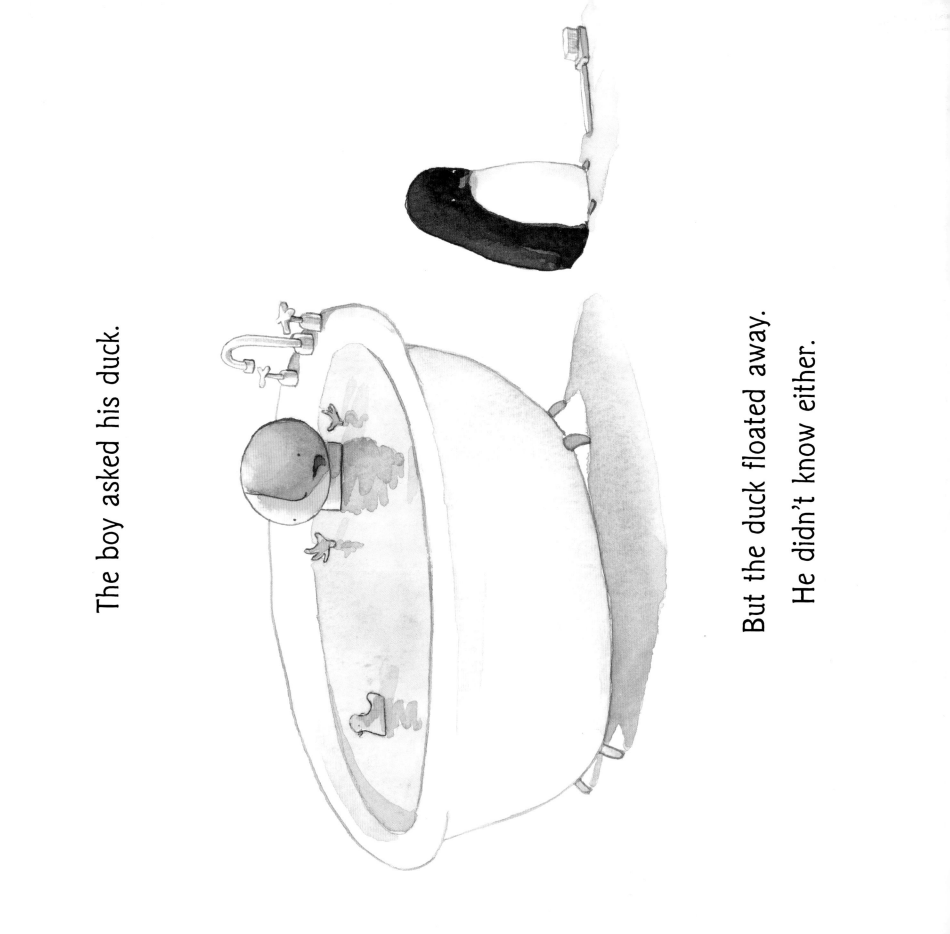

The boy asked his duck.

But the duck floated away.
He didn't know either.

That night, the boy couldn't sleep for disappointment. He wanted to help the penguin but he wasn't sure how.

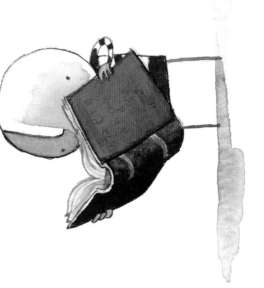
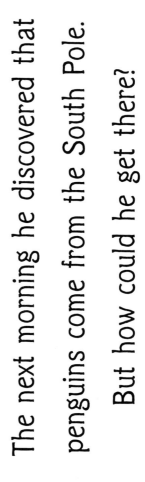

The next morning he discovered that penguins come from the South Pole.

But how could he get there?

He ran down to the harbor and asked a
big ship to take them to the South Pole.
But his voice was much too small
to be heard over the ship's horn.

Together, the boy decided, he and the penguin
would row to the South Pole.

So the boy took his rowboat out and
tested it for size and strength.
He told stories to the penguin
to help pass the time.

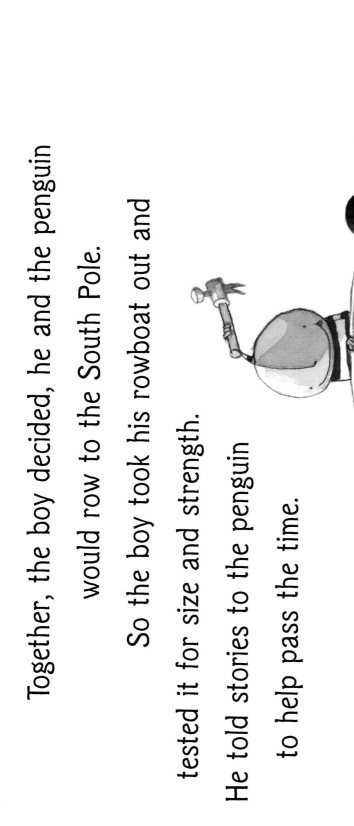

Then they packed everything they would need . . .

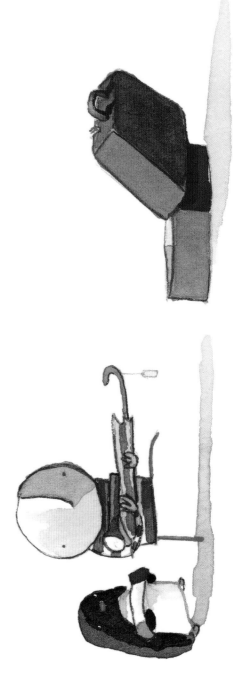

. . . and pushed the rowboat out to sea.

They rowed south for many days . . . .

. . . and many nights.

There was lots of time for stories, and the penguin listened to every one, so the boy would always tell another.

They floated through good weather and bad,

when the waves were as big as mountains.

Until, finally, they came to the South Pole.

The boy was delighted,
but the penguin said nothing.
Suddenly it looked sad again as
the boy helped it out of the boat.

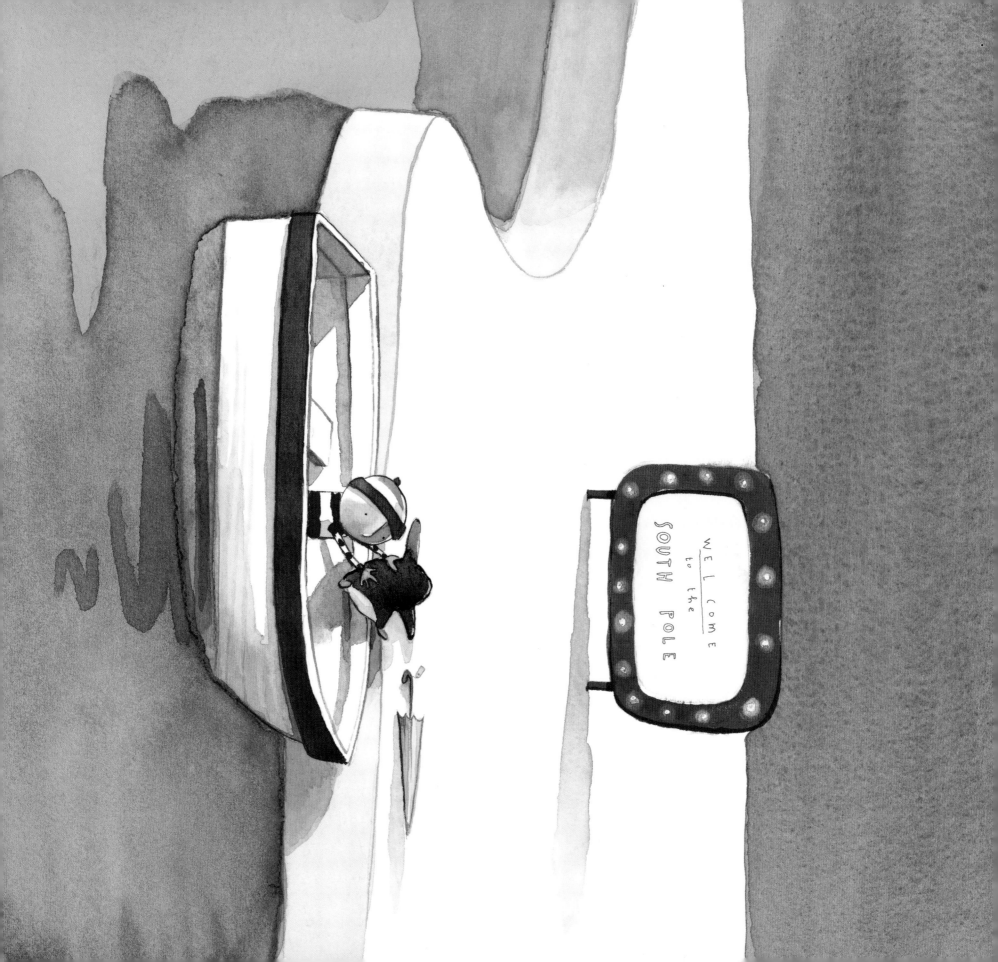

Then the boy said good-bye . . . .

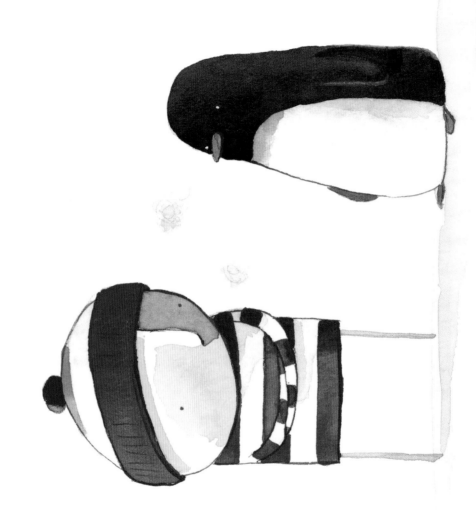

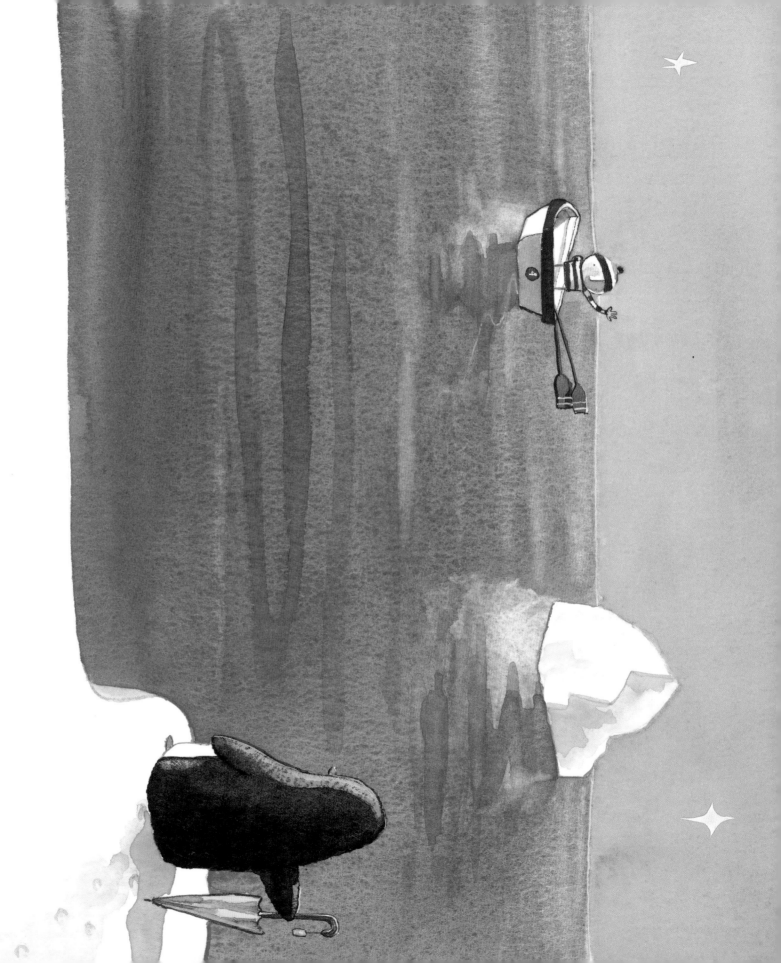

. . . and floated away. When he looked back, the penguin was still there. But it looked sadder than ever.

It felt strange for the boy to be on his own.

There was no point telling stories now

because there was no one to listen

except the wind and the waves.

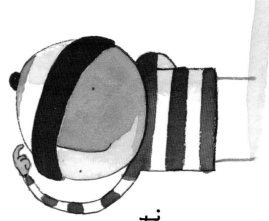

Instead, he just thought.

And the more he thought . . .

. . . the more he realized he had made a big mistake.

The penguin hadn't been lost. It had just been lonely.

Quickly he turned the boat around
and rowed back to the South Pole
as fast as he could.

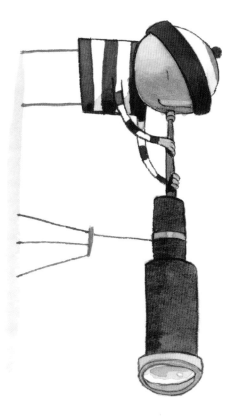

At last he reached
the Pole again. . . .
But where was
the penguin?

The boy searched
and searched, but
he was nowhere
to be found.

Sadly, the boy set off for home.

But then the boy saw something
in the water ahead of him.

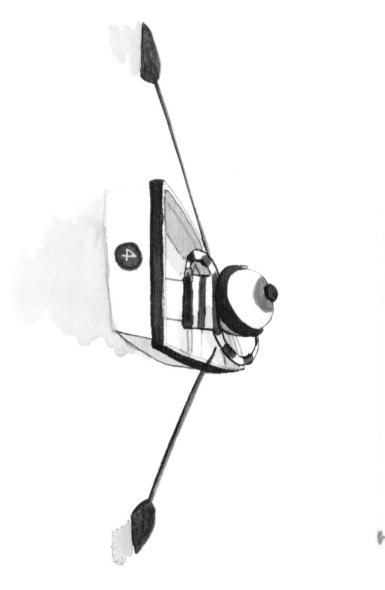

Closer and closer he got,
until he could see . . .

. . . the penguin!

And so the boy and his friend went home together, talking of wonderful things all the way.